Emma,

"blues

Weighting On Love

Sophie Blue

Copyright © 2020 Sophie Blue

All rights reserved

The characters and events portrayed in this book are fictitious. Any similarity to real persons, living or dead, is coincidental and not intended by the author.

No part of this book may be reproduced, or stored in a retrieval system, or transmitted in any form or by any means, electronic, mechanical, photocopying, recording, or otherwise, without express written permission of the publisher.

Cover design by: Sammi Bee Designs
Edited by: Magnolia Author Services

Contents

Title Page	1
Copyright	2
Dedication	7
Chapter 1	9
Chapter 2	13
Chapter 3	19
Chapter 4	22
Chapter 5	27
Chapter 6	33
Chapter 7	36
Chapter 8	40
Chapter 9	46
Chapter 10	50
Chapter 11	55
Chapter 12	58
Chapter 13	65

Chapter 14	68
Chapter 15	72
Chapter 16	75
Chapter 17	78
Chapter 18	82
Epilogue	86
Curious about Kyle?	91
Acknowledgements	93
What Are You Weighting For?	97
About The Author	99

Dedication

To anyone who has ever felt less than perfect. You were born to be real, not perfect. You are perfectly imperfect. You are unique. And you deserve everything.

Chapter 1

Liam

At thirty-two, I'm one of the youngest gym owners in the country. I love my job. Fitness has always been important to me, and I enjoy helping other people achieve their fitness goals too. Setting up my own gym was the icing on the cake. *What Are You Weighting For?* is my baby. I own it, I run it, I live it. Spacious, modern, and open, it's quickly becoming one of the most popular gyms in the country. With state-of-the-art machines and highly qualified trainers, my gym is one of the most sought after, and I couldn't be prouder.

Making my way through the open white space of the main room to my office, I offer a nod to Kyle as I pass him giving an induction to a new member. Kyle has been with me since the beginning and is my best mate. He's a pain the neck most days, but he's also one of the best trainers at the gym with a huge waiting list.

I'm almost at my office when I see a cute brunette looking like a deer in headlights. I hear her whisper

"This was a mistake" before turning to make a swift exit. But in her haste, she fails to notice the six-foot-two man standing in front of her and smacks straight into my toned chest.

"Can I help you?" I ask, catching her before she falls backwards and taking in her pained, embarrassed face. She clearly does not want to be here, but wow, she is stunning. Long brunette hair pulled back into a tight ponytail, curves to make a monk weep, and chocolate coloured eyes that I could easily lose myself in.

"No, thank you; I should go." She tries to run past me, but I'm quicker, and I'm not done. I've lost count of the amount of people who have walked through the door and bottled it. I gently keep hold of her arm and try to put her at ease. She must have come here for a reason.

"You didn't come all the way here to take one look and leave, did you?" I smile cheekily, hoping to break the ice. "This is my gym. I'm Liam."

"I'm Chloe." She shyly smiles back. "But I don't belong here." She frowns, but it doesn't make her any less beautiful.

"How so?" I ask, trying to figure out this woman. She's beautiful, curvy in all the right places, and hidden under baggy clothes. The sad smile on her face makes me want to slay her dragons. My sister has a similar expression when she is upset, and it always makes me feel like I'm taking a sledgehammer to the chest.

"Seriously? Look around! This place is full of gorgeous, skinny people and I look like I got lost on my way to the cake shop," she murmurs, mortified, her cheeks pink in embarrassment.

"First off, don't ever say that again. You're beautiful. And people get fit by coming here. All these people? They probably started in the same position as you," I reply, annoyed that she's putting herself down. Too often today, people are so quick to label themselves and each other. The world can be tough enough without us turning against ourselves.

"I doubt that," she scoffs, looking at her feet like a schoolgirl being told off by the principal. It's endearing as hell. What is wrong with me? She's a potential client who needs some reassurance, not some creep eyeing her up like a sweet treat at a bakery.

"Look, we close at six-thirty pm today. Why don't you come back then, and I can give you an induction when it's empty? Maybe that will make you feel more at ease?" I find myself asking, not sure why, but I want to help her. Fitness helps me, and I like passing that on to others.

"You don't need to do that. I'm just wasting everyone's time." She sighs, looking close to tears and hiding behind the strands of her brown hair that have come loose from her ponytail.

"No you aren't. I'd like to help you. Please? Let me show you that this place isn't so scary." I shoot her another encouraging smile, hoping it puts her at ease and reassures her that I'm not the enemy.

"Ok, thank you," Chloe whispers, looking up at me with a shy smile. *Focus, Liam.*

"My pleasure. I'll see you at six-thirty," I say, shooting one last smile her way, I turn and finally make my way to the office, closing the door behind me. Today just got a lot more interesting, that's for sure.

Chapter 2

Liam

"Glad you came back." I smile down at Chloe as she makes her way into reception looking slightly less frazzled than when I'd seen her earlier. She's in a pair of leggings and a baggy t-shirt, with a hair tie around her wrist ready to workout.

She looks embarrassed again. "Thanks again for being so kind," she offers, clutching her water bottle like it's a security blanket.

"Don't mention it," I reply, leading her to the office and offering her a seat in front of my desk. I grab my blood pressure monitor off the shelf and lean back against my desk. "I just need to take your blood pressure; do you mind?"

She shakes her head and holds her arm out for me to attach the cuff. I put the monitor on the desk and start the machine, watching the cuff inflate around her arm. As the pressure releases, I take note of the reading and remove the cuff from her arm, returning it to the same shelf. "Perfect, we're good to go."

"So why did you decide to join the gym?" I ask as I take the seat across from her, picking up some forms and a pen to record her details, noting down her blood pressure. Paperwork is my least favourite part of the job, but it has to be done.

"Operation Flirty Thirty" she replies bashfully, playing with the hem of her light blue t-shirt.

"I'm sorry?" I grin, looking up from my desk, not sure I heard her correctly. She is adorable, sitting across from me, looking the picture of innocence with her flushed cheeks and biting her lip.

"I turn thirty next year, and I want to be the best me when it comes around," she offers with a shrug of her shoulders.

"Ok, so you want to get fit and tone up?" I clarify, writing it down as we speak. Not an uncommon goal, and definitely something I can help with.

She scoffs. "I want to not be fat and frumpy at thirty."

"You're not fat and frumpy. Don't say that," I find myself scolding, not liking how she keeps putting herself down. The world is cruel enough as it is without people criticizing themselves.

"His words, not mine," she mutters and looks away, trying to focus on anything other than me.

"Whose words?" I ask, ready to punch them in the mouth. Who speaks to a woman like that?

She looks up, shocked that she said it out loud. I find her lack of filter endearing, but that won't distract me.

"No one's. So where..."

"Whose words, Chloe?" I insist, not letting her off the hook so easily. I watch her shift in her seat uncomfortably and then sigh.

"Michael, my ex. He was less than complimentary when I found out he was cheating on me. Said it was my fault for having let myself go and embarrassing him," she mumbles, going red and looking close to tears.

"Sounds like Michael was a prick." I answer with complete sincerity. Who the hell did her ex think he was, treating a woman that way? If a guy ever said something like that to my little sister, Molly, I'd break every bone in his body.

She laughs, a real belly laugh, and it's the best sound I've ever heard. She is stunning when she smiles; I want to see her do it more.

"What kind of an arsehole cheats on his woman and then blames her?! The guy is a prick, and you're better off without him," I continue, and Chloe smiles up at me, a beaming genuine one that does things to me. She is beautiful. How can she not see that?

"Thanks. But still, he wasn't wrong. I have let myself go and, I want to get back on track and be proud of my body," she says, straightening her shoulders and looking determined for the first time since I've met her. "I used to be slimmer, more confident. I mean, I was never happy with myself, but who is?"

I nod. I have a lot of members whose focus is improving their weight and figure. Nothing beats seeing a true transformation happen; that's why I became a trainer. It's a rush to see someone discover what their body can do and how they can harness that power and reinvent themselves.

"Ok, so why don't we go and have a look around, I can show you the machines and weights, and we can come up with a program for you. How does that sound?" Putting the paperwork down, I stand and motion to the door that leads back out into reception.

"Perfect, thank you so much!" She smiles, standing to follow me as I make my way through reception and into the main area, pulling her long hair back into a ponytail.

***

I take my time showing Chloe around each of the

machines, making sure to explain their purpose and how to use them. I can tell she's anxious, but I take it slow, trying to help her feel more comfortable. A lot of people feel intimidated by gyms, using equipment wrong because they're too embarrassed to ask for help. That's how injuries happen, so inductions for new members are non-negotiable. Better to be safe than sorry.

While helping her off the cross trainer, I ask, "What do you think? Are you up for a trial? I can make you a program..."

She bites her lip again, looking far too appealing. "I don't know. I want to, but what if everyone laughs at me?" Her brow is furrowed, she is genuinely concerned. I hate that her ex has done such a number on her.

"Firstly, no one will laugh at you. Everyone has their own motives for being here and are too focused on that to take notice of others. Secondly, anyone so much as looks at you wrong and I'll speak to them." I say with sincerity, giving her shoulder a reassuring squeeze. I don't tolerate bullying or bitchiness in my gym.

She giggles and looks up at me with the cutest smile. "Thank you for being so kind; you have no idea how much I appreciate it." Her eyes shine with candour, and I have to remind myself to take a breath. *What the hell is wrong with me?*

"You're welcome. I'm glad I could help." I answer honestly, not knowing why I feel so drawn to her, but I truly want to help her achieve her goals. I tell myself it's the overprotective big brother part of me coming out to play, but I know that is bull.

We walk back to my office, and I give her a membership card along with a list of the opening times and some paperwork for her to read through and keep.

"Monday and Thursday evenings tend to be the quietest, if that's what you'd prefer."

"That would be great, thanks!" She smiles and grabs her bag, swinging it over her shoulder, and heading towards the door behind me, looking slightly more at ease than she did when she arrived, which pleases me to no end.

"Drive safe and hopefully I'll see you soon." I wave her off and shut and lock the door once she's safely driving away.

Fuck. What was that about? I've never opened late for a client, never given a free induction and never lusted after a client like I had after Chloe. She's trouble with a capital T. And worse, she has no fucking idea.

Chapter 3

Chloe

I wake up feeling determined. Liam had been amazing and patient showing me around all the machines and explaining how they worked and what part of the body they'd target. I find myself feeling optimistic that I can actually do this. I can lose forty pounds and show Michael what he's missing. I'm feeling motivated and ready to kick butt! It doesn't hurt that my trainer is practically a god and looks like Liam Hemsworth...

After dragging myself out of bed and taking a hot shower, I make myself a healthy breakfast of wheat biscuits with yoghurt and strawberries. Grabbing my cup of coffee in my *Central Perk* mug and my breakfast, I walk over to my sofa and take a seat, flicking through the copy of *Women's Health* I'd picked up earlier in the week. Liam says I can do this. I can totally do this.

***

Later that night...

Ok, it's official, I can't do this. Only five minutes on the treadmill and I already feel like I'm going to faint. I'm a sweaty mess, out of breath, and think I may pass out. Turning the treadmill to a walk, I try to catch my breath so I can walk out with my head held high and never return. Just as my pulse starts to come back down, it spikes again as Liam walks my way.

"Hey Chloe, good job. How are you getting on?" he asks with a disarming smile, leaning up against the wall to my right. With his tight white vest stretching across his impressive chest and black shorts, he's quite a sight. I need a minute to remind myself that he asked me a question.

"Terrible. This was a waste of time. I'm a mess," I reply, quietly and in a defeated tone that I notice is becoming my norm. I hate that this is who I've become. My face is so flushed, I'm half expecting Santa to come barrelling through the door mistaking me for Rudolph.

"It's day one, Chlo; what did you expect? It won't be easy, nothing worthwhile ever is. But stick at it and I promise you'll see results." He promises, giving my trembling hand a reassuring squeeze. I look around nervously, seeing all the other members working out and using the machines like pros.

"No one is looking at you sweetheart; they're focused on their own workouts. You've got this." He soothes me, offering a reassuring smile that elevates my heart rate again.

I send him a watery smile, "Thanks. Have a good night." Deciding I'm done, I stop the treadmill and get off, grabbing my water bottle and heading to the changing room.

"Why don't you come back tomorrow evening after closing, and I'll take you through your programme?" Liam calls out as I try to make a run (ha, who am I kidding? I don't even run to catch a bus) for it.

I turn and look up at him, "You really don't have to do that. You've already been too kind to me." I don't want him to pity me, no matter how much of a mess I am.

"I want to. I know you can do this, I want to help you believe that you can too." He gives me another one of those charming smiles. It really isn't fair how he can do that! Is there anyone on the earth with the power to resist that smile?

"Ok, thank you." I send a genuine smile his way in return. "I'll see you tomorrow then."

"Have a good night. And good job today." He complements as I wave and head back to the changing room. Liam is right, this is only day one. I can do this.

Chapter 4

Liam

Sitting at reception so I can keep an eye on the main door, I'm catching up on my paperwork when Kyle makes his way out of the main room of the gym and stops in front of the long, white desk.

"You heading out mate?" I ask, putting my pen down and stretching my arms over my head to soothe my aching shoulders. Today has been manic.

"Yeah, hot date tonight!" He waggles his dark eyebrows at me with a stupid grin on his face. Of course he has a date; he's our town's answer to Casanova. With his jet-black hair and muscular physique, he's very popular with the ladies. Ironically, I'd told him it was fine as long as he keeps it professional at the gym. And here I am obsessing over a client.

I chuckle, standing and making my way around the desk, playfully punching his shoulder. "Have a good one." I swear this guy gets laid more than a rock star, lucky bastard.

His attention lands past the front door as he says,

"Looks like I'm not the only one with a date tonight." Mischief is dancing in his dark blue eyes.

I follow his gaze and see Chloe making her way through the near empty car park.

"Behave; I'm helping her with her programme," I chastise, not sure if I'm trying to convince myself or him. I've never offered after hours training sessions before, but something about Chloe triggers my protective side. I see how terrified she is of people mocking her or looking at her. Her arsehole ex has really knocked her confidence. She is a beautiful woman, no matter what weight she is. She clearly wants to improve her health, and I want to help. I love the gym. Few things give me a high as good as the one I get after a good workout, and I love helping others achieve that feeling too.

"Sure, man, whatever you say." He smirks, slinging his designer duffel bag over his shoulder and heading for the door. "Have a good night."

I shake my head at him and chuckle; he can be such a jerk. "You too, don't forget to wrap it up." He gives me the finger and a grin as he holds the door open for Chloe, nodding hello as he passes her.

"Hey, how're you doing?" I ask, walking towards her and locking up once she is safely inside.

"Good, thanks. How was your day?" She smiles,

much more at ease now we are alone. It's like she is a different woman. Her black leggings and baggy 'Joey doesn't share food' t-shirt do nothing to hide her beauty.

"Busy, but good, thanks. You ready to get started?" I ask, while leading her into the large main room and pointing to the other side where the state-of-the-art treadmills are.

"As ready as I'll ever be!" She sighs, giving me a cheeky smile. Grabbing the hair tie from her wrist, she makes quick work of securing her hair behind her. I am definitely not imagining myself running my fingers through it. *Nope.*

We walk over to the treadmill, and I set her up for a brisk walk to start warming her up. People underestimate just how important a warmup is.

"So, tell me about you," I say, increasing the pace of the treadmill ever so slightly. I lean against the wall and cross my arms over my chest.

"What about me?" she asks, clearly surprised by the question.

"Anything. What do you enjoy doing? What are your goals? What TV shows do you like binge watching?" Though judging by her t-shirt, I have an idea on that last one. While I am genuinely interested in her answers, I'm also trying to take her mind off of the workout. You'd be surprised how many people struggle with working out just because they keep focusing on the fact that they don't want to do it.

"I love reading, and my goal is to be successful in my floristry business. And I like binge watching *Friends*. I'm a tad obsessed with it." She pants, turning a bit pink at the increased tempo of the treadmill.

"Good answers! Kinda figured with your t-shirt," I joke. "And which *Friends* character are you most like?" I increase the incline slightly on the treadmill.

"Monica in high school." Chloe snorts, reaching for her water bottle and taking a swig.

"Chlo, stop it. Seriously, which character?" I ask, frustrated at her constant put downs. I check my watch to see how long she has been going and monitor her progress.

"Probably Phoebe. I'm a bit quirky, I'm happy with my own company, and I have absolutely no filter. Who would you be? You've got to be Joey, right?" She pants, keeping up the pace.

"Why's that?" I ask, looking up and curious as to her thinking.

"Because you're hot and must get all the girls." Chloe flushes, realising what she has just said. "See, no filter."

I laugh. "It's cute. Ok, enough of the warmup, let's pick up the pace."

"What? This is still the warmup?" she cries, looking alarmed. I try and fail to hide my grin; she really is something else.

Chapter 5

Chloe

To say I've had a tough day would be an understatement. Work was manic, running my own florist is amazing, but some days are too much. With the wedding season approaching, orders are sky high. and I don't think I've had a spare minute all day. I'll be seeing lilies and roses in my sleep.

Speaking of weddings, I received an invite to my cousin's wedding when I got home. My cousin who first introduced me to Michael, as they are uni friends. Then my mother called to warn me that Michael and his new girlfriend have also been invited. Cue meltdown. Not only will I have to face the man who broke my heart in front of my family, but I'll also have to do so looking frumpy in comparison to his new girlfriend. The one he was screwing while we were still together. Life is cruel.

So after demolishing the packet of Oreos from the kitchen cupboard and half a share bag of Kettle Chips (Only half! Winning.), I'm now lying on my sofa in my *Friends* PJs feeling sick and sorry for myself. I rummage around in my bag and find the business card Liam gave me, sending him a quick text to let him know I won't be there for our session this evening. No use in embarrassing myself even further.

Text sent, I scroll through a takeaway app on my phone to order a pizza (why not? I've already fallen off the wagon, might as make the most of it) when it starts ringing in my hand. It's Liam. *Shit.*

"Hello?" I answer sheepishly, feeling like a naughty schoolgirl about to get a detention. *Why did you pick up, you muppet!*

"Chloe? Are you ok?" he asks, sounding concerned, making me feel even more guilty for ditching him. *The guy is keeping his gym open late for you Chlo, and you go and stand him up!*

"Yes I'm fine, just can't make our session tonight. Sorry." I cringe at how lame I sound, hoping he'll drop it.

"How come?" he asks, no anger in his tone, just curiosity.

"Something came up..." I find myself stuttering pathetically. Could I be anymore awkward?

"Uh huh... what's that?" he replies in amusement, clearly not buying it for a second and amused by my obvious discomfort.

"Um, I have to wait in for a handy man to sort me out?" I phrase it as more of a question than an explanation and bang my head against the coffee table in mortification. *Think before you speak, Chlo!*

"Lucky guy." He chuckles. I can feel my cheeks flaming. "What's really going on Chlo?" he asks, sounding genuinely concerned.

I sigh. "I got an invite through the post for my cousin's wedding. My mum rang to warn me that Michael is also invited, as is his new girlfriend. So I turned to junk food, stuffed my face til I felt sick, and now I'm sitting here feeling sorry for myself and about to order a pizza, because clearly I haven't binged enough," I rattle off in record timing. Bet he is sorry he asked now!

Liam is silent.

"Are you still there?" I ask, wondering if he had hung up on me in disgust. I wouldn't have blamed him.

"Yep. Still here. Want someone to share the pizza with to half the damage?"

"You want to come over for pizza?" I ask, confused but secretly delighted that I'll be able to ogle him somewhere besides the gym.

"If you don't mind? I could use some dinner, and we can discuss your plan."

"Plan?"

"To knock Michael's smile off his face when he sees the new you walk into the room at the wedding."

I giggle (who on earth giggles?!) and rattle off my address. This night has just got a damn sight better.

***

I jump when I hear the doorbell go, not knowing whether Liam or the pizza has arrived first. We'd agreed on a Hawaiian pizza and garlic bread—he has good taste. People who don't think pineapple belongs on pizza have no idea what they are missing. Although, how Liam can eat pizza and still look like he does is a mystery to me. Some people have all the luck.

I get up from my spot on the sofa, do a quick once over the living room to make sure my mad dash to tidy it has been sufficient and open the door, doing a double take. Liam in gym gear is sexy AF. But Liam in jeans? Holy moly.

"Hey." He smiles that adorably charming smile, and I step back to let him in. Jeans that fit his arse to perfection, a leather jacket, and a fitted black t-shirt that shows off his muscles, combined with a killer smile. How is this god of a man stuck spending his night with me?

"Hey. Pizza should be here any minute," I reply, feeling shy all of a sudden. I've swapped my *Friends* PJs for a pair of leggings and a red and white spotted dress, but I still feel self-conscious next him.

"Awesome, I'm starving," he replies, taking his jacket off and making his way to the sofa. He puts his jacket over the back and sits down, making himself at home.

"So, let's talk about the wedding," he says, looking up at me expectantly.

I am taken aback for a moment. "What about it?" I ask as I sit on the other end of the sofa and turn the TV down where season five of *Friends* is playing away to itself.

"When is it?"

"In twelve weeks. I think." I had only skim read the invite earlier, too busy catastrophising to take in all the details.

"Then we have twelve weeks to work on the new you. That's a doable time frame. I can make you a program. Stick to it and trust me, and I guarantee you will blow Michael away."

I'm dubious. "Have you seen me? Short of lipo and a facelift, I find that highly unlikely." I laugh awkwardly.

Liam isn't laughing, "We need to address this, Chlo. You're a beautiful woman. How can you not see that? A few extra pounds can't take that away from you. And this guy is an arsehole for making you feel that way."

I blush and look down. I feel Liam gently grab my chin, forcing me to look at him.

"You are. Don't let him take that away from you. Twelve weeks, and you're going to walk into that wedding a different person. Mark my words."

I smile. "Skinny Chloe!"

"Confident Chloe," Liam corrects, dropping his hand and smiling at me. "Confidence is the sexiest thing a woman can wear."

Judging by his face, I must look sceptical.

"I'm serious, Chloe. There is nothing sexier than a confident woman who is comfortable in her own skin. Weight... that's just a number. You are so much more than just a number."

Who is this guy and how is he so swoon-worthy?

Chapter 6

Chloe

After our heart to heart over pizza the other night, I walk into the busy gym with my head held high, my headphones in, and the playlist to end all playlists playing through my phone. I am going to do this. Fudge you, Michael.

I go into the changing room, put my things away, and head to the treadmill with a water bottle and said killer playlist to start the warmup.

Halfway through my workout, I see Liam out of the corner of my eye. He is helping another member. A woman. A gorgeous, blonde, toned, slim, woman. I catch myself frowning, which is ridiculous. I have no claim on Liam, and it is literally his job to be nice and help people. That woman isn't special. And neither am I. So why does that make my heart sink?

***

Liam

I'd seen Chloe come in and get started on her work

out. I am proud of her for starting to come to the gym during regular hours. I don't mind the private evening sessions at all; they are fast becoming the highlight of my week, and I have no intention of stopping them, but it's good that she's starting to get more confident in her abilities and being around others. She's making good progress and looks in the zone today.

Once I've talked a member through an exercise she is struggling with, I look over at Chloe. Something has changed in the past half hour, that much is clear. Gone is the determined woman who'd entered the gym earlier, and in her place is a disheartened woman. Her pace has slowed and she looks moments away from bolting.

I head over to her and lean up against the treadmill she's on. Seeing me, she reaches up and pulls a headphone out of one ear.

"You ok, Chlo?"

"Yeah, good thanks." She flashes a brief, fake smile that doesn't reach her eyes.

Something is definitely up. "You sure?"

"Yep, thanks," she says, picking up her pace and putting her headphone back in. Guess this conversation is over then! I give her one last look before going to do my rounds, trying to decipher what is going through her head. This woman is a mystery that's for sure, but lucky for me, I'm an excellent detective. Game on.

Chapter 7

Liam

It's after hours, and I'm helping Chloe through her programme again. It's become our norm and something I look forward to each night. We get on like a house on fire, and I love her quirky sense of humour. She seems to have bounced back after her dip in confidence at the gym the other day, and I am proud of her progress.

Heading to the mats in one corner of the vast open space, I point to the floor. "Let's get down on the mat and do some core exercises." The machines are great and definitely effective, but I like to do a lot of mat work and introduce exercises that clients can do at home. The easiest way to create a plan people will stick to is to create one they can do anywhere at any time. No excuses about not being able to make it to the gym.

Chloe groans, looking like a stroppy teenager who has just been told to clean their room. "Or... we could just say we did?"

She really is something else, and I can't help but chuckle. I love her sense of humour. It isn't going to distract me though.

"Get on the mat, Chlo." I point again, putting my hands on my hips to show I mean business.

She snorts. "Ok, you don't have to go all dom on me."

Who the hell is Dom? "Huh?"

"You know, 'get on your knees baby,'" she mimics in a deep voice, snorting to herself.

I'm speechless. This shy, self-conscious woman is sure as hell full of surprises. I can see the colour flooding to her cheeks as she realises what she's just said. God bless her lack of filter.

"Well, we can start there if you want." I laugh. "But I usually suggest we start with you on your back." I throw her a wink and a cheeky grin. She looks like she wants the ground to swallow her whole and fuck if that doesn't make my dick twitch. She is too adorable.

I talk her through a circuit of ab cycles, Russian twists, and reverse crunches before sending her off to do her cool down. As she walks away, I find my gaze following her amazing backside, and not for the first time. *Focus man!*

"So I was thinking, how about tomorrow we meet at yours at six am and go for a run?"

"Sure! And after, we can jump on a space shuttle and take a tour of the moon," she says, grabbing her water bottle and rolling her eyes as if I had suggested something completely ludicrous.

I cock a brow at her, waiting for her to explain once she's finished rehydrating.

"A run?" She scoffs. "I don't think that is such a good idea."

"Why's that?" I ask, amused by the look of pure horror on her face at the mere suggestion. You'd think I'd suggested a picnic on top of an active volcano.

"Because I like living? I get out of breath running up the stairs. Running isn't a strength of mine, and I'd rather not subject the general public to my attempts."

I chuckle, unable to stop myself from teasing her. "Why's that? Do you run like Phoebe?" I ask, alluding to her favourite TV show.

"Ha, no. She's too fast for me. I'm more like a disorientated snail with respiratory problems." She snickers.

"Now this I have to see," I say through a laugh. Walking with her to the main entrance and unlocking the door, I say, "I'll see you at six am."

"Seriously Liam, I can't run." She is starting to panic, I can tell. Running is the enemy to most people.

"Yes, you can; I've seen you on the treadmill. Relax, we'll take it slow. I'll see you tomorrow. Good job today," I end the conversation so she knows I won't back down, giving her one last smile as she leaves in an adorable huff, muttering to herself. After locking up, I head back to my office to finish some bits and pieces off. Living next door to the gym has its advantages. I can be home in five minutes and don't have to worry about traffic.

Chapter 8

Chloe

I must have done something awful in a past life. Why else am I being punished like this?

True to his word, Liam turned up at my front door at an ungodly hour, looking sinfully gorgeous. It isn't fair. How can he roll out of bed and look like a cover model, whereas I look like a blowfish in spandex who's been dragged through a hedge backwards? I genuinely feel awful. I may have overindulged slightly in a takeaway last night to combat my dread for this morning. To make a bad situation worse, I explained my dire need for a caffeine fix first thing, but he said we'd stop for a coffee after. Cruel. So cruel. Who deprives someone of *coffee*?

"You're doing great, Chlo. Let's pick up the pace a bit," the handsome devil says, jogging backwards next to me, making it look far too easy in his designer running gear. Meanwhile my lungs are burning, and I'm pretty sure my heart is going to jump out of my chest and chastise me for putting it through such torture.

"This is the only pace I have, unless you want to walk. I am totally down for walking," I gasp out whilst attempting to keep moving. I heard someone say once that the worst thing you can do is stop as you won't be able to get started again.

Liam laughs gently and picks up his pace, "Quicker we go, sooner you get a coffee."

Smart man! I pick up my pace and focus on that cup of hot, sinful, caffeine-filled goodness that I am going to devour once I make it through this cruel and unusual punishment. I just pray I survive!

***

Liam swings the door to the coffee shop open and motions for me to go in first. The smell of fresh coffee hits me as I enter, and I sigh in relief. Well, gasp in relief, still trying to catch my breath. Is there anything better than the smell of coffee? Apart from drinking it, obviously!

I join the queue and debate what I'm going to have. So much caffeine goodness lay before me; this is my happy place. And don't even get me started on the cake counter. Yum!

Liam joins the queue behind me and takes out his leather wallet, "What are you having?" How does he look so put together? I feel like my legs might give way underneath me, and he is standing here looking like he is auditioning for a commercial.

"A skinny flat white, but I can get it," I reply, averting my gaze from the amazing display of calorific goodness in front of me. *I do not need cake. I do not need cake.*

"No, my treat. You did good today," he says, throwing another one of his charming smiles my way that has me melting into a pile of goo.

I laugh a completely unladylike laugh that has a few people in the queue turning to look. Or maybe it is my snort that draws them.

"I barely kept up with you, and you looked like you were practically walking!" I reply, shaking my head.

"You never stopped, Chlo; you went the whole twenty-five minutes without stopping, and you couldn't have done that a couple of weeks ago, could you?" He asks, grabbing a bottle of water from the display and leaning against the counter.

"No, I guess not," I admit. I may not be marathon ready, but I have just jogged further than ever before. I guess that is progress. Liam smiles; he seems proud, which does something to me.

Once we reach the front of the queue and get our order (a cup of heaven for me and a bottle of water for him) we head back out. I give one last fleeting look to the baked goods section, mourning my loss.

As we reach the door, I hear a high-pitched female voice say, "Liam?"

Liam and I both turn and are greeted by a tall, slender blonde woman who looks like she has stepped off of the cover of *Vogue*. She's wearing a skin-tight purple jumpsuit and a pair of Jimmy Choos.

"Nadia, hey. How are you?" Liam asks, obviously no stranger to her. *Of course he isn't.*

"Good, thanks. You look as gorgeous as ever! How is the gym going?" she purrs, touching his chest with her perfectly manicured hands like she's trying to stake her claim.

"Good, thanks. It's going good," he replies, the pride evident in his voice.

She glances over at me, only just noticing he isn't alone, and looks at me like a piece of gum stuck to her ridiculously expensive heels.

"Oh, Nadia, this is my friend, Chloe. Chlo, this is Nadia." Liam realises his faux pas and introduces us, unaware of his friend's obvious distain for me.

"Hi." I wave like an idiot and she gives me a fake smile.

"Hello." She gives me a once over and must decide I'm not a threat. She leans in to kiss Liam on the cheek. "Let's have dinner soon; it's been far too long."

And with that, she turns on her stupid heels and is on her way. I'm definitely not hoping she slips and falls on her perfect, stuck-up arse on the tiled floor and wipes that stupid smile off of her perfect face. Nope. Not me.

Liam, oblivious to the pissing contest that's just occurred, motions for me to exit and follows me out, taking a swig of his water.

"So, Nadia? Is she an old flame?" *Smooth Chlo, really bloody smooth.* I internally face palm as I await his response.

"Nah, not really. She used to train with a buddy of mine from the gym, Kyle. We hung out a few times. Nothing serious though." *Hung out? Is that what the kids are calling it these days?* I snort at my own stupid joke, and Liam raises a brow at me. Busted.

"Sorry. She seems… nice?" I phrase it as a question.

"Forget about her. So what are your plans for the rest of the weekend?" he asks, conveniently changing the subject. I groan, remembering what I have to do. Maybe dying from that run wouldn't have been such a bad thing after all.

"I have to go dress shopping for the wedding." I screw my face up at the thought. Clothes shopping when you're not the size you want to be sucks. Do you try the dress on that you want to fit and be crushed when it is too tight? Or do you pick a bigger size to be safe and then get upset when it fits perfectly even though you tell yourself you're definitely not that size? Nothing about clothes shopping appeals to me. I'd rather lick a cactus, thank you very much.

"Want some company?" Liam asks. I stop abruptly and he almost bumps into me. "What?"

"You'd come clothes shopping with me? Isn't that a guy's idea of hell?" I ask, puzzled by his offer.

He chuckles. "I guess, yeah. But I don't mind. I get to see you try on pretty outfits." He winks at me and I blush, feeling my whole body heating up.

"Believe me, it's nothing to write home about." I mutter, thinking back to his supermodel friend.

Chapter 9

Chloe

Three dresses later and I'm starting to despair. Nothing looks good on me and that isn't just me exaggerating. Dress one made me look like Violet Beauregarde from *Charlie and the Chocolate Factory*, dress two made me look like an extra in a period drama, and the less said about dress three the better. I can't find anything to compliment my shape, and I may be having a slight meltdown in the fitting room.

"Chlo, I got another one," Liam says from outside the door. He's being a trooper, bless him. Opening the door to my cubicle, I let him in. He's holding a gorgeous royal blue dress.

"That won't fit me," I say in embarrassment, glancing at the tag attached.

"Try it on," Liam insists, handing it to me unrelentingly.

"Liam, it isn't my size! It won't fit." I cry in despair. How can he not see how awkward this is? I'm too big for the dress and trying to pull it on would be mortifying.

"Chloe, trust me. You've been working your butt off these past few weeks; your body is changing. Just try it, ok?"

With his ocean blue eyes fixed on mine, I reluctantly agree. Sighing, I take the dress off the hangar. "Ok, will you wait outside?"

"Sure." He smiles in triumph, leaving the room so I can attempt to change into his selection. I flip the lock and turn away from the mirror. No use bearing witness to this.

I undress and start to slip into the beautiful blue dress, waiting for the moment it gets stuck and for the mortification to set in.

It doesn't.

The dress slides on with relative ease, much to my surprise. I slowly turn to look at myself in the mirror and gasp at my reflection. It looks good. *I* look good.

I hear a knock on the door, "You ok in there?" I flick the lock so he can come back in. He closes the door behind him and turns to take me in.

"Wow, look at you!" He smiles, a genuine beaming Liam smile that melts my heart.

"It fits." I smile, not sure when I last fit into a dress this size. I'm proud of myself. It hasn't been easy, but I've worked my backside off for this. I deserve this little victory.

"Told you so," he says with a smug look. If he wasn't so hot, I'd want to slap the arrogant look off his delectable face.

"Thank you" I say, truly meaning it. He's slowly giving me back what I lost. My body. My confidence.

"It's just a dress Chlo." He shakes his head humbly while putting his hands in the pockets of his jeans.

"No, not just the dress. For being so nice to me, not letting me flee the gym that first night even though I must have looked quite a sight, offering me private sessions to put me at ease, taking my sarcastic comments in your stride, never giving up on me even when I wanted to give up on myself. Just... thank you, for everything." I give him a shy smile and squeeze his hand.

Liam smiles back, tucking an errant strand of hair behind my ear. He starts to lean in toward me. I think I stop breathing as I watch in slow motion as his lips approach mine. No way this is happening? No freaking way.

Knock, knock. "Is everything ok in there?" The sales assistant calls through the door. *Are you freaking kid-*

ding me?!?

Liam jumps back and looks bashful. "I should go," he says, reaching for the door, "You look great, Chlo!"

The door closes behind him and I fall against it. What just happened?

Chapter 10

Chloe

After our almost kiss (if I didn't imagine the whole thing), I pay for the blue dress and we part ways. So tonight is the first time I'm seeing him after the incident, and I have decided to pretend nothing has happened. That way it won't end in embarrassment if I have fabricated the whole thing in my overly dramatic head. After all, I spend most of my time with my head in a romance novel, so I wouldn't put it past myself to have started blurring fiction and reality.

Liam meets me at the door to the gym with his usual friendly smile. "Hey, how're you doing?" he asks, locking up after me and following me to the main room.

I chuckle. "Good, thanks, Tribbiani. You?"

He laughs at my lame joke. "I'm good. It's been busy today, lots of new members, which is always good. Do you want to get started on your stretches and I'll go turn the music on?" he asks whilst already walking toward the sound system.

I head to the mats and start my warmup routine, my favourite part of the workout as it doesn't make me feel like I'm going to die. By the time Liam has made his way back over, I've jumped on the treadmill and started the second part of my warmup.

"Nice Chlo, you've got a good pace going already," he encourages, leaning up against the wall. "So how was the rest of your weekend?"

"Not too bad. Got some errands done, tidied the house, binge watched *Friends* whilst drinking copious amounts of coffee. You know, the usual." I smile. "How about you?"

He chuckles. "Sounds good to me. Not much, caught up on paperwork, worked out, same old," he replies, shrugging as he increases the incline on the treadmill.

"Eurgh, you spend all week at the gym. How can you come here and work out on your day off?" I ask, looking at him in horror. He is clearly a masochist.

He laughs. "I enjoy the rush it gives me. Plus I don't have to come far. I live in the house next door."

"You know, in my experience, cake also gives the same effect." Grinning, I wink at him.

"Alright smart arse, let's take it up a notch." He

laughs, increasing the speed of the treadmill. "So are you all set for the wedding now that you have the dress?"

"I guess. I mean, I'm pleased I found it, but I'm still dreading going." I admit through strained breaths. The thought of facing Michael and his new girlfriend makes me feel sick to my stomach. I'd never eat cake again for the rest of my life if someone would just uninvite him. *Just kidding. If you're listening, God, please don't take my cake away.*

"Can I ask you a serious question?"

"Of course," I say, glancing over at him and noticing his earnest expression.

"Why are you going to this wedding?"

I furrow my brow at him. "It's my cousin's wedding. I have to go."

"No, you don't. You said yourself, you're not close in the slightest. It's making you anxious just thinking about going. Why tie yourself up in knots?"

"I can't drop out of the wedding, Liam. For one, it's rude. My mother would be livid. And two, it gives Michael too much credit. It makes it seem like he is getting to me."

Exasperated he lifts his hands into the air in disbelief. "He *is* getting to you! You're working your backside off five days a week and for what? To show him what he's missing and win him back?"

"What? No! I don't want him back. I just want him to see that he shouldn't have discarded me so easily after I gained weight. I deserved better than that." And I finally see that now.

"You do deserve better than that. Which is why I hate how much power you put on his opinion. Clearly the guy is an idiot for letting you go."

I don't know what to say to that, so I don't. I let the silence stretch out between us. The only noise is coming from the music playing in the background, my laboured breathing, and the thud of my feet on the treadmill.

"You're so much more than you realise, Chlo. I just wish you had the confidence to see that."

"Thank you," I whisper. No one has ever said anything like that to me before.

"Look, I'm going to a fundraiser next week. My gym donates every year. Would you like to be my plus one? Call it a dress rehearsal for the wedding," Liam says with a cheeky grin, trying to lighten the mood again.

"Really? You want me to go with you?" I ask, sure I must be mistaken. There's no way Liam Hemsworth's twin brother is asking me to accompany him out in public. Not when he can have any date he wants.

"Yeah. It'll be fun and it will be a good practice run for you." He's smiling as he increases the speed of the treadmill again.

"That does sound fun," I reply, attempting to smile even though I'm now panting like a dog in the summer. "I'd love to go with you."

Chapter 11

Chloe

The past couple of days are spent thinking about what Liam had said about the wedding. Why *was* I going? I'm sure my cousin wouldn't notice my absence. I'd like to think he'd understand why I feel uncomfortable attending considering the circumstances. After all, blood is thicker than water, right?

After grabbing a fresh cup of coffee from the kitchen, I pad back into the living room and grab my phone off of the coffee table. Thinking it over for a little while longer, I finally dial my mother's number and wait, trying not to hold my breath, unsure of how this conversation is going to go.

"Hello darling, I was just thinking about you," my mother answers, in her usual sunny demeanour, which makes me smile.

"Hi, Mum, are you ok?" I ask. We speak at least once a day via text. My mum is my best friend.

"Yes, love. I'm just looking for a dress for the wedding. Your dad is wearing the suit he wore to Marie's wedding last year. Men have it so easy!" She moans, and I can just imagine her shaking her head in frustration.

Sighing, I get straight to the point. "Mum, I don't think I'm going to go to the wedding." Silence greets me as I wait for her to digest my announcement. I sit down on the sofa and take a sip of my caffeine courage.

"Why on earth not?"

"It is going to make me uncomfortable seeing Michael there with his new girlfriend. I just don't think I'm ready. I don't want to have to face the pity on people's faces or deal with the questions that might get thrown my way."

"Chloe, this is your cousin's special day. It's about him, not you. I think you're being very selfish," Mum replies in an annoyed tone that I recognise from when she chastised me as a child.

"Mum, it isn't selfish. We aren't that close; I'm sure they'll understand. They'll probably be grateful to avoid the atmosphere." Closing my eyes, I plead that she'll understand where I am coming from. She knows how broken-hearted I was after what happened.

"Chloe, enough. You're being silly. This isn't about you. It's just one day. Put a smile on your face and come celebrate with the rest of your family!" She isn't hearing what I'm saying, and I am starting to get frustrated and upset.

"No, Mum. I can't. Please send them my apologies, I'll send them a card…"

"Chloe! You're…" I cut her off, losing my temper. She is supposed to be on my side! I'm her daughter, for goodness sake.

"Mum, he broke my heart. Shattered it into a million pieces and then blamed me. He blamed me! I'm not going to sit across from him and smile, pretending that seeing him and his floozy isn't like receiving hundreds of papercuts to my heart. I'm not going, I'm sorry. And that's it." I hang up the phone and scream at the ceiling. Why can't she see how uncomfortable the situation would be for me?

Chapter 12

Liam

Another manic week done, and I am nursing a cold beer on my sofa, flicking through channels. I'd invited Kyle over for a lad's night but he, shockingly, has another hot date. Standard Kyle.

Scrolling through Netflix to find a film, I hear the doorbell ring and frown, making my way to my front door. I'm not sure who to expect at this time of night; I can't imagine Kyle would be done so soon, the night is still young, and he can't have had a chance to suit up yet, surely? Swinging the door open, I am not ready for the sight that greets me.

Standing in the pouring rain, brown hair stuck to her face, with mascara running down her cheeks, is Chloe. And fuck, she has never looked more appealing than in this moment.

"Chloe? Are you ok?" I ask, concern evident in my tone, as I glance over her to see if she is hurt. What on earth has happened?

"You were right. I put too much weight on other

people's opinions of me. No pun intended." She throws me a sad smile, her tear-filled eyes glistening in the faint light of the evening. "I shouldn't be trying so hard to please people. It's like that *Friends* episode where Monica overhears Chandler call her fat and she makes it her mission to lose weight to shove it in his face. But she stabs his toe and…"

I cut her off, aware that she's still standing in the pouring rain and clearly having a bit of a meltdown. "Come in, you must be freezing." I pull her inside my apartment and shut the door, locking up after her. I turn to look at this woman who's turned my life upside down in such a short space of time.

"My whole life I've felt big. Never happy with my size or appearance. And do you know what? It's exhausting. I'm exhausted, Liam. I can't keep trying to become someone I'm not meant to be."

"You don't need to be anyone but you, Chlo. You're perfect," I state with the utmost sincerity. This woman has no idea how extraordinary she is. She always has been.

"I wouldn't go as far as perfect, but you know what? I'm me. And I'm healthy and happy and I'm done trying to be anything else," she says, smiling up at me, a genuine smile like she's had an epiphany and finally believes in herself, like I have all along.

I can't help myself. I pull her towards me and crush

my lips to hers. She is a vision. Even dripping wet with messed up makeup, she is stunning. Confidence suits her.

Her arms make their way around my neck and she pulls herself closer, moaning delicately into my mouth. She is ice cold and getting my clothes wet, but I couldn't care less. She's perfect. This is perfect. I press her against the wall as one hand makes its way under her soaking wet hoodie.

I pull back with a start, realising how cold she must be. "Let's get you out of these wet clothes," I say, taking her hand and leading her up the stairs to my bedroom. Once inside the navy blue room, I turn on the light, letting go of her hand reluctantly to rummage through my drawers in search of something she can wear. "Did you want to jump in the shower to warm up?" I ask, looking over my shoulder at her. She is biting her lip and I lose all train of thought except for that I want to be the one biting that lip.

"Isn't there another way we could get warm?" she whispers with a combination of innocence and sin that's spellbinding. I grin at her and stalk towards her like a predator. Backing her up to my bed, I pull her wet hoodie over her head and throw it behind me. Checking her face to make sure she's onboard with this, I make quick work of her t-shirt whilst she removes her shoes, hanging on to my shoulder for balance. I'm unbuttoning her jeans when she stills my hand with hers, and I look up into her eyes.

"You ok?"

"Can we turn the light off?" she requests, her insecurities making their way back. I don't want the light off, I want to see every inch of her beautiful body. But I want her relaxed more than anything.

"Sure," I say. Anything to make her more comfortable. After flicking the switch, I turn my bedside lamp on to give the room a soft glow and go back to removing her jeans. Wet denim is officially the devil!

Finally, she is standing in front of me in only her lacy black underwear, and I am blown away. This woman is something else.

"You're so beautiful, Chlo," I whisper, kissing her neck and pulling her against me so she can feel exactly what she is doing to me.

"You make me feel beautiful," she moans back, moving her hands under my shirt to pull it off. I help her get rid of it and pull away to make quick work of my jeans.

"How are you even real?" she whispers, touching my chest and tracing the muscles she finds there. Like I'm a treasure map and she wants to explore every inch.

I smile down at her. "I was just thinking the same thing," I say before taking her mouth again. I will never tire of the taste of her lips. She's addictive. A mix of coffee and Chloe. Pure sin. She lowers herself to my bed and I have to take a moment to appreciate the view. Her in my bed. Chloe in my bed. Fuck, if that isn't the hottest thing I have ever seen.

"Are you sure this is what you want? We don't have to do anything tonight if you don't want to," I offer, even though I can feel my cock trying to tunnel its way out of my boxer shorts. *Jeez, calm down before you embarrass yourself, buddy.*

"Are you kidding? I've been fantasizing about you from the moment we met!" she replies, before dropping her head back to the pillow and slapping a hand to her mouth in embarrassment. God, I love her lack of filter.

Grinning wickedly, I kneel over her on the bed, tracing the edges of her bra with my fingers ever so gently. "Oh really? And what happened in these fantasies?" I ask, kissing her nipples through her lace bra and drawing a loud moan from the deity laid out in front of me like an offering to the gods.

"Can we just forget I said that?" she gasps, hiding her face behind her hands as I trail kisses down her body, making sure I explore every part of her smooth skin.

"Not a chance in hell." I chuckle, looking up at her from where I now sit, between her thighs. "I love your lack of filter."

She groans and I'd like to think it is less to do with my statement and more to do with the fact that I've just slipped my fingers into her knickers. Fuck, she is drenched.

"Oh, fuck! Liam!" she gasps, her fingers clutching onto the duvet and arching her back.

So she has a potty mouth as well as a lack of filter? Good to know.

I increase the tempo of my fingers and use my other hand to unhook her bra. She is still coherent enough to slip the straps down her arms and discard it; clearly I need to work harder. *Challenge accepted.*

With one hand still pleasuring her, I lean forward and take one of her pink nipples in my mouth. She has the most perfect breasts, and I am looking forward to getting well acquainted with them. As I gently bite down, she groans with pleasure and pulls my hair.

"Fuck, Liam!" She writhes under me like she can't get enough, and damn if that doesn't stroke my ego. I smile into her cleavage and pull back to watch her fall over the edge, riding my fingers.

"You ok?" I ask, as she is catching her breath, smiling down into her gorgeous brown eyes. She smiles and pulls me down into a slow, lingering kiss.

"I'm better than ok," she whispers, pulling me back down with a sexy grin. She doesn't need to tell me twice.

Chapter 13

Chloe

I wake up and roll over to check my clock for the time, only I'm not in my bed. I look around, taking in my surroundings and remember that I crashed at Liam's last night. When we eventually crashed…

I can't stop the smile from stretching across my face as I turn to the other side of the bed and see the man himself, lying next to me looking like a cover model for one of those romance books I love to read. He is gloriously naked, having pushed the duvet off of himself at some point in the night and I can't help but take him all in. He really is insanely hot. He starts to stir and when he opens his gorgeous blue eyes and spots me, a lazy grin spreads across his handsome face and reaches his eyes.

"Good morning, beautiful Did you sleep well?" he asks whilst stretching his arms out and giving me a glimpse of those well-earned muscles at work.

"Yes, thanks. I haven't slept that well in forever." I smile back. Feeling shy all of a sudden in the cold light of day, I pull the duvet further up my body to cover myself.

"Don't hide from me, Chlo. I've already seen and explored every inch of you. I know you're gorgeous." A salacious grin appears on his face as he thinks back to the previous night's activities.

Blushing, I loosen my grip slightly, watching as he sits up and checks the time.

"Ok. Let's get up and get a morning run done before breakfast. Burn some calories," he says with a grin, moving to get out of bed.

"Or... we could stay in bed and find another way to burn some calories?" I offer, grabbing his muscular arm before he leaves the bed completely.

He turns and smiles down at me. "Whatever happened to that shy girl who showed up at my gym?" he asks with a cheeky grin and a hard on that says he is a BIG fan of my alternative plan.

"She's still here, she just *really* doesn't want to go for a run..." I reply with a sheepish grin, and he barks out a laugh before rolling back over me and forgetting about his morning run.

"What am I going to do with you?" He chuckles, biting my lip gently and drawing a soft moan from me.

"I have a few suggestions..."

Turns out there are some workouts I enjoy!

Chapter 14

Liam

We are halfway through Chloe's warmup, but she seems distracted this evening. Her head seems to be somewhere else.

"Everything ok?" I ask, handing a bottle of water to her while taking a swig of my own.

"Huh? Oh, yeah." She smiles, coming out of the deep thought I lost her to just moments ago.

"You sure? Your head doesn't seem to be in the game today." I smile, walking over to turn the music down.

"Can I ask you a weird question?" she calls after me. I turn to take in her nervous expression. Her black leggings cling to her like a second skin and the form fitting vest she is wearing makes me lose track of my thoughts for a minute. Especially since I know what treasure lies beneath it now.

"Of course. What's up?" I focus again, making my way back to her. I pull up a gym ball and sit down in front of her, leaning my arms on my thighs and waiting to see what is on her mind.

"Have you ever had sex in the gym?" It's a good thing my balance is on point, otherwise I'd be flat on the ground right now. *Did she just ask me what I think she did?*

"I'm sorry?" I bite out, chuckling and taking in her flushed cheeks.

"Of course you have. Sorry. That was an incredibly inappropriate thing to ask," she scolds herself, turning away from me in embarrassment.

I have no idea where this has come from or what is bothering her, but she should know the truth. "No, Chlo. I've never had sex here. I don't mix business with pleasure. I mean, I never did before…" I trail off; clearly we are past just professional now.

An adorable smile spreads over her face as she turns to me. "Really?" she asks far too enthusiastically.

I chuckle. "Yeah, really. Where did that come from?" Taking a swig from my water bottle, I wait for her reply.

"Last night I dreamt I sucked you off here, and it was kind of hot," she blurts out. *Thank you, Chloe's lack of filter!*

I choke on the gulp of water I've just taken and look

at her in disbelief. "What?"

"I dreamt…" I am on her in an instant, discarding my bottle. Gym ball bouncing away, forgotten. Fuck professionalism. It is my gym, I make the rules. There is nothing sexier than a woman who is confident enough to make the first move. I cup her cheek as I devour her mouth, wanting to claim every inch of her. This woman is driving me crazy in the best way possible. I pull back to take a breath and she drops to her knees. Holy fuck!

Chloe has my shorts and boxers pulled down in no time and wraps her small hand around my aching cock. I throw my head back with a groan when she applies just the right amount of pressure and starts jerking me off. She smiles innocently at me before leaning forward and taking me in her mouth. The warmth of her mouth combined with her motions has me reaching for her hair and wrapping my hand in it. Checking her expression to make sure she's ok with the direction this is taking, I tighten my hold on her hair when I hear her moaning. Fuck, innocent Chloe likes it a bit rough. Could this woman be any more perfect? I pull her hair a bit tighter and thrust into her willing mouth, throwing my head back in pleasure when I feel myself hit the back of her throat.

"Fuck, Chlo, I'm about to explode," I warn her, expecting her to pull back. She doesn't. Pulling me deeper into her throat again, she hums around my cock, squeezing my balls, and I'm a goner. My release comes before I can pull back and she swallows every last drop, only pulling back to lick her lips once I'm spent.

Still on her knees looking like a goddess, she grins devilishly up at me. "Protein's good when you work out, right?"

Fuck. Me.

Chapter 15

Liam

Pulling into Chloe's drive, I switch off the engine and check my hair in the rear-view mirror. I've never taken a date to a fundraiser before, but I'm really looking forward to tonight. Spending time with Chloe is always the highlight of my week. She is truly something else and I love her company (not to mention her body). After we spent the night together last weekend, we have barely been apart except for when we are working. I open my door and climb out of my car, walking up to her door and giving a swift knock on the wood.

The door opens and it is like time stands still. Chloe stands at the door wearing *the* blue dress and looking breath-taking. I have to remind myself to breathe.

"Wow. You look amazing, Chlo," I manage to get out and her smile is everything. She's curled her long brown locks and used a darker shade of lipstick than normal, accentuating her lush lips. Her eyelids even have a light dusting of blue on them to compliment her outfit. It takes all my willpower not to push her back inside and devour her like an animal. What this woman does to me!

"Thanks. I thought I'd give the dress an outing, considering I won't be wearing it to the wedding now." She smiles, looking nervous and playing with her black clutch. It still blows my mind how she is oblivious to her appeal, but her innocence is disarming.

"It's stunning, just like you. Are you ready to go?" I ask, holding out my hand for her and thanking my lucky stars that I stopped her from bolting out of the gym that day.

"As ready as I will ever be," she replies, taking my hand and closing her door behind her, making sure it is locked before letting me lead her to my car.

"Confidence, Chlo. It's all about confidence, remember? You're a beautiful woman. Own it."

She gives me one of those breath-taking smiles and I'm done for. I reach out to cup her cheek, moving a stray wisp of hair from her face. Slowly, I lower my lips to hers and there are fireworks. This woman blows me away. I've never reacted to anyone the way I do to her. When I finally pull away, I smile down at her, keeping my nose pressed to her forehead.

"I've been waiting to do that all day." I admit, smiling down at her and then continuing to my car. Let's get this show on the road, sooner we get there, sooner we can leave…

Chapter 16

Chloe

Ok, this isn't so bad. I do feel good in my new dress, and everyone seems friendly. Liam has introduced me to a few of his friends and talked me through what the fundraiser is for. He has donated a year's gym membership to the auction and some personal training sessions. Everything I learn about this man only makes me like him more.

I'd slipped away from Liam to visit the ladies' room, but not before he checked in with me to make sure I was ok. He really is perfect. After reapplying my lipstick, I leave the room in search of my hot date. MY date. The smile on my face is going to have to be surgically removed at this rate.

***

Liam

Chloe seems to be having a great time, and so am I. These fundraisers aren't usually something I look forward to. Contrary to my larger than life appearance, I'm not a huge fan of mass gatherings. But with

Chloe here, I am actually enjoying myself. We have such a laugh together. She is a breath of fresh air, and I'm glad she is starting to feel comfortable in her own skin.

My buddy Nick and I are catching up over a beer at the bar. He runs a sports clothing store and I am always sending business his way and vice versa. We've been friends for years. My sister used to have the biggest crush on him in school. I can't tell you how relieved I was when she got over that. Not because he's a bad guy, just because he has a reputation not too far off Kyle's.

Midway through a conversation about the shenanigans at our last barbeque, I feel someone tap on my shoulder and turn around, expecting to see Chloe. But I'm surprised to see Nadia standing there with a scowl on her face instead.

"I didn't have you down as a chubby chaser," Nadia sneers, her bright red lips screwed up in distaste. How did I ever find this woman attractive?

"You're dating her?" Nick pipes up, always eager to get the latest scoop.

"I'm not a chubby chaser," I bark back at Nadia, trying to rein in my temper. Who the hell does she think she is, talking about Chloe like that?

I hear a gasp and turn around. Chloe stands there,

looking pale and hurt. My heart sinks.

"Nice, Liam, real nice," she says, her eyes filling with tears, before she turns and makes a hasty retreat.

"Fuck!" I shout as I run after her, not giving a shit if I'm making a scene. Perfect fucking timing.

I make it into the street in time to see Chloe jumping into the back of a taxi. Fuck! This is not happening! Running to the car park, I jump into my car and start heading for her house.

***

Pulling outside Chloe's house, I park and hurry up her path to the door, pounding on the wooden frame.

Either she isn't answering and is sitting in the dark, or she hasn't come home. *Fuck*. What has just happened? I went from having everything to having nothing in the space of one evening.

Chapter 17

Chloe

When I jumped in the taxi, I gave the driver the first address that came to mind: my parents'. My safe place. That's how I find myself stood outside the front door of their modest terraced house ringing the doorbell. I think to myself how ironic it is that I am here again, crying on my parents' doorstep after a man broke my heart. It's almost like I've come full circle in the last few months. First Michael, now Liam.

Mum opens the door and smiles when she sees it's me, the smile quickly being replaced with a worried frown when she sees my tear stained face.

"Chloe? What's wrong, sweetie?" I fall apart, throwing myself into her arms like I'm a small child seeking comfort again. The soothing smell of her perfume engulfs me and makes me feel safe. She is quick to usher me in out of the cold, whispering words of reassurance as she closes the door and leads me to the living room.

Collapsing on her chocolate coloured leather coach, I am quickly pounced on by her black Labrador, Rover. I give him a big hug and scratch him behind the ears while he licks my face like I am his everything. *At least someone cares about me*, I think sardonically.

"What's happened, Chloe?" my mum asks, coming in and sitting beside me while taking my hand. "Carl, make your daughter a coffee," she shouts through to the kitchen to my dad.

Good old Mum, she knows the way to my heart. Coffee is the answer to everything. I take a deep breath and launch into it, "I joined a gym after the Michael fiasco. I met a guy, a personal trainer. He was handsome and charming and supportive. We got close and I thought… I thought he really liked me. He said all the right things, listened to me, we had so much fun together." I smile through my tears, and Mum squeezes my hand.

"What happened, sweetheart?"

"We went to a fundraiser together tonight. He introduced me to his friends; I thought everything was going really well. I went to the ladies' room and when I came back I heard one of his friend's ask if we were dating." I choke out the last bit, fresh tears starting to flow at the painful memory. "He said he wasn't a chubby chaser," I cry out. Mum pushes

Rover out of the way and gives me a cuddle. "I really thought he liked me, Mum, but he was just like Michael."

My dad walks in with a mug of coffee and hands it to me, giving me a reassuring smile and leaving us to it. He isn't great with big emotional displays, but I know he'd be there if I asked him to be. Rover follows him out, upset he is no longer the centre of attention.

"What did he say when you confronted him?" Mum asks, sitting back and taking a sip of her coffee.

"I didn't. What was there to say? He made it crystal clear how he felt." I sniff, wiping my nose with the tissue Mum hands me and sniffling.

"Chloe, you should have given him a chance to explain. It may have been a misunderstanding," she gently chastises, patting my hand.

"What was there to misunderstand?? He sees me as an overweight woman who was easy to get into bed!" I cry out, slurping my coffee like it may evaporate at any moment.

"Firstly, you're beautiful, sweetheart. How many times do I have to tell you that?" I go to tell her that she has to say that, but she cuts me off with a wave of her hand. "You are beautiful and by the sound of this man, he wouldn't struggle to find a willing woman. Am I right?"

"Yeah, I guess"

"Then why would he just use you as an easy lay, if he could get one of those anywhere? Talk to him, Chlo, see what he has to say. If you don't like it, don't see him again. Just make sure you have all the facts before you make a decision you may end up regretting."

I think about what she is saying. I guess that does make sense. But why would he say that? I sigh. "How did you get so wise?"

"I'm a mother, it is part of the job description." She laughs. "And I owe you an apology, sweetheart. You were right. If it makes you uncomfortable, you shouldn't go to the wedding. It was unfair of me to try and guilt trip you into going. I'm sorry."

I lean in and hug her, a proper bear hug. No matter what happens, she's always there for me. My greatest supporter and my best friend.

"Thanks, Mum." I whisper.

Chapter 18

Chloe

After staying at Mum and Dad's last night and talking it through with Mum, my voice of reason, I get a lift back to my place with Dad, turning my phone on before I get out of his car and saying goodbye to him with a kiss on the cheek.

Letting myself in the front door as Dad pulls away, I throw my bag down on the floor and check my messages. I have five missed calls from Liam and two texts. I open them up while heading to the kitchen to make some coffee.

Please talk to me Chloe, it's not what you think.

I'm sorry, please call me.

Grabbing my coffee and my phone I make my way to the sofa and try to figure out my next move. Mum is right, I can't shut the door on whatever it is we have without hearing him out. Whatever he has to say, I need to hear. I message him back, *I'm home now, if you're free and want to talk.*

His reply is almost instant. *I'm on my way.*

I throw my head back against the sofa and sigh. Nothing is ever simple.

***

Twenty minutes later I hear the doorbell and go to let Liam in. He looks like crap. Well, as crap as a god-like creature can look. He clearly hasn't slept much, if at all, and I feel a bit of remorse for rushing out on him. But then I remember what I'd heard and strengthen my resolve. I'm not in the wrong here. He is.

"Chlo…"

"I thought you were different, I thought you really liked me," I whisper, feeling less confident now that he's standing in front of me and I have to face his truths.

"I do! Please, just let me explain…" He reaches out to touch me, but I step back out of his reach as the floodgates open.

"I heard you, Liam! Your friend asked if you were dating me and you said you weren't a chubby chaser with disgust in your voice!" I shout, my calm resolve disappearing. I may not be in his league, but how dare he treat me like that! "All that crap about not being defined by my weight, was that all a line?

Make the fat girl feel good so you could get her into bed and have a good laugh about it with your friends?" I cover my face, finally feeling my resolve start to crack as the tears start to appear.

"No! No. Chlo, you only heard half of the conversation. Nadia had called me a chubby chaser first; I was responding to her, not Nick. I'm not a chubby chaser because you are perfect, and YOU are the only woman I'm chasing. Your weight IS just a number! I don't care what size you are, Chlo. I never did! I offered you private sessions from the very start, I invited myself round for takeout because I was drawn to you. It doesn't matter whether you weigh two hundred and thirty pounds or one hundred and thirty pounds, I'm crazy about YOU."

I peer up at him through my fingers, "What?"

"I'm crazy about you, Chlo. You must be able to see that?" He leans down in front of me and gently takes my hands in his. "Catching you before you ran out of my gym was fate. You are everything I want."

"That's insane. Look at you! You're practically Liam fudging Hemsworth!"

"Stop!! You are beautiful. Inside and out. You're kind and caring and loyal and funny and determined and sweet and honest and stunning and have *absolutely* no filter. And I want to spend every day telling you that. If you'll let me." He reaches up and cradles my cheek in his warm hand, and I lean into his soft touch.

"For real?" I squeak, not sure if I'm dreaming.

"For real." He grins. "You're my lobster, Chlo. The Monica to my Chandler, the Rachel to my Ross. The..."

I cut him off by jumping into his arms and kissing him with everything I have.

Epilogue

Liam

Is it hot in here, or is it just me? I feel like I'm on fire. I'm not used to being nervous, but today I am bloody terrified. Sitting in my office, I'm a bundle of nerves, and it's a feeling I'm not familiar with. Nor do I welcome it.

It has been eight months since Chloe and I became 'official.' Life couldn't be any better. I love my job, the gym is going from strength to strength, and I love going home every night knowing Chloe will be there waiting for me. I'd convinced her to move in with me once her lease ran out a couple of months ago. Nothing beats waking up to her every morning and falling asleep by her side every night.

Today is the day I am going to propose. I'd spoken to her parents and received their blessing, I'd picked out a ring that I thought she'd love, now I just have to pop the question. Why do they say that? 'Pop the question' like it's no big deal. Just another question to slip into conversation like 'Oh hey, can you pass the sugar?' or 'Baby, did you want pasta tonight?'.

And now I'm rambling, see! Nervous.

Kyle walks past my office and backtracks when he sees me at my desk, poking his head in. "You ok, buddy? All set to pop the question?" *Gah!*

I drop my head to my desk in despair. Are my palms sweating?

"What's up?" Kyle asks, making his way in and dropping into the seat in front of my desk.

"What if she says no? What if she thinks it's too soon?" I feel like a teenage girl gossiping, but I need my best mate right now. I'm losing it.

"Liam, that girl is obsessed with you. God knows why. She didn't even bat her eyelashes my way, so it must be the real deal," he jokes, throwing a teasing grin my way. "You've got this! Just don't overthink it. It's going to be fine."

He's right, I can do this. I take a deep breath and sit up, getting the ring box out of the desk drawer to my left and looking at it again. It's eighteen-carat white gold with a round cut diamond solitaire in the centre. Understated elegance the saleswoman had said, and I knew it would be perfect for my girl.

"It's beautiful, mate, she is going to love it." He stands, offering his fist to me, which I bump in gratitude, "Now stop being such a wet blanket and go get yourself a fiancée!"

I laugh, watching him leave. Chloe will be here shortly. We still have our evening sessions once she finishes work, before we go home together. I want to propose in the first place I laid eyes on her. So here I am, getting ready to tell the woman I love that I want to spend forever with her. *God, I hope she says yes.*

***

Chloe

Parking outside our house, I make my way to the gym and let myself in with the key Liam had made for me. The first thing I notice is the lack of light in reception; that's odd. The only light illuminating the large room is the spotlight above the reception desk.

"Liam?" I call out, wondering where he is. He usually meets me here before we get started. I begin to make my way to his office but before I get too far, I see him make his way out of said office and stand next to the reception desk looking a little uneasy.

"Are you ok?" Walking towards him with concern, I stop when he meets me halfway.

"This is where I first laid eyes on you." I smile, remembering our awkward first meeting. "I took one look at you and just knew I was meant to help you. You were so lost and afraid, and I wanted to save you. But that's not what happened." I look at him in confusion; that is exactly what happened. Liam brought me back to life.

"You saved yourself, Chloe. You proved to yourself that you're capable of anything. You stood your ground, you worked your cute arse off, you showed up to every session and gave it your all. And you realised just how amazing you are and what you're capable of. I am in awe of you, Chlo. You are everything I never knew I needed. And I want to spend the rest of my life showing you just how worthy you are."

My heart stops when I see him sink down onto one knee. *Oh. My. God.* Great, here Liam is being romantic as hell, and I was channelling my inner Janice!

"Will you make me the luckiest man alive and marry me?" Opening a velvet ring box to show the most stunning ring I've ever seen, he looks up at me with his signature grin.

"Yes! A thousand times, yes!" I throw myself at him and we fall into a heap on the floor laughing. I don't know what I did to deserve this man, but I do know that together, we are perfectly imperfect. And I couldn't be happier.

Curious about Kyle?

Pre-order his story now!

Fighting For Love – Coming Soon!

US Pre-order

UK Pre-order

Acknowledgements

To my husband, thank you for your unwavering support, for loving me despite my book obsession and for being my best friend. You mean the world to me.

To my parents, thank you for always telling me to follow my heart. I wouldn't be the person I am today without your constant love and support.

To Sarah from SWBR Graphics, not only for creating the most amazing graphics and teasers, but for being a wonderful friend. I'm so grateful to have you in my life.

To Sam from Sammi Bee Designs, thank you for helping make my vision a reality. I adore my beautiful cover and couldn't have done this without your support.

To Brooke, thank you for being my cheerleader and not laughing when I told you I was writing a book. Here's to another 25 mad years!

To my beta readers, thank you for your kind words of support and for taking a chance on me. It means everything.

Finally, to the light of my life. Always follow your dreams baby. You can do anything you set your mind to.

And thank you to YOU for taking a chance on my book. I hope it made you smile.

What Are You Weighting For?

Series

Weighting On Love

Fighting For Love

Running From Love

About The Author

Sophie Blue

Sophie Blue is a hopeless romantic and avid romance reader. She fell in love with reading at a young age and can always be found with her nose in a book. She started writing after having her baby and is enjoying creating worlds to get lost in.

How to keep in touch:

Facebook – www.facebook.com/sophieblueauthor
Instagram – www.Instagram.com/SophieBlue-Author
Twitter – www.twitter.com/SophieBlueAuth
BookBub – www.bookbub.com/profile/sophie-blue
Goodreads – www.goodreads.com/SophieBlue-Author

Printed in Poland
by Amazon Fulfillment
Poland Sp. z o.o., Wrocław